Sir Johnny's Recycling Adventure

Closing The Recycling Loop

Girl Scout 100th!

Dear Christina Hughes)
Happy Earth Day 2012
Rachel Paulson

Hands On The World Books

Crestmont Publishing
Sparta, New Jersey

CREDITS

Design	Paragon Media
Executive Editor	Jackie Hutto – j.h. public relations
First draft editing	Debbie Meyer
Second draft editing	Author Dianne Ochiltree
Editorial support	Mirna Rosende, Andrea Elliker, Cathy Hayes, Kathi Cullen, and Christine Reedy
Photography	Peter Sharp – Sharp Images
Marketing	Shine & Associates

Special Thanks To:

John Hildenbiddle	For your positive energy that spreads like wildfire to those who know you. Thank you for sharing your spirit with me.
Carolyn Merritt	Who opened doors and inspired the subject of this story upon our first meeting.
Jackie Hutto	Who is always there at the perfect time.
Colleen Shine	From start to finish you traveled with me each step of the way. It has been a great journey. You really do shine!
The Roselle Family	My friends – and support system.

Acknowledgments

A million thanks to Champion International Corporation for making this project possible. Champion is truly committed to educating children about our environment. Through their involvement with my books, thousands of children have been motivated to help make a difference in our world. I am proud to work with such a company.

Rachael Paulson

Thanks to the American Forest & Paper Association (AF&PA) and the 100% Recycled Paperboard Alliance for their support. Thanks also to AF&PA for providing the educational information and activities in the back of this book. AF&PA encourages teachers to copy and distribute those pages for educational purposes.

Dedicated to my sweet children, Danielle and Mikey,
and my very patient husband Mike.

Written in memory of my brother Johnny.

Printed and bound in the United States
Published by Crestmont Publishing
7 Highview Road, Sparta, NJ
by arrangement with Champion International Corporation
Copyright ©1999   Rachael Peterpaul Paulson
Library of Congress   99-93535
ISBN   0-9642296-2-5

There once
was a boy
named Johnny,
who loved
everything
about the
Earth.

1

More than anything,
he loved the giant old
oak tree in his very own
backyard. Its strong branches held a magnificent
tree house built by Johnny's dad. It was a special
place that brought his imagination to life.

There will be no climbing today, thought Johnny as he looked up at the slippery, snow-covered landings of his tree house. Johnny stood beneath the huge white oak, his arms filled with old newspapers and magazines.

Carefully balanced on top of the stack of papers sat a periscope. Johnny had made it himself from an empty cereal box just this morning. He was ready for adventure on this cold winter day.

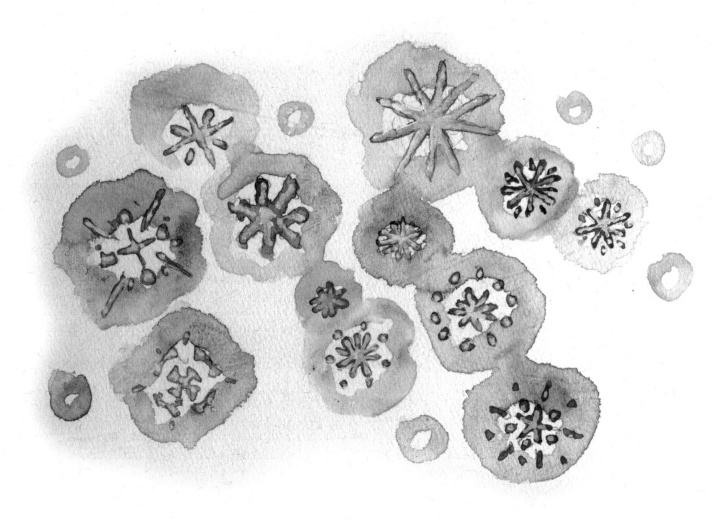

"Good morning, Tree," said Johnny,
brushing snowflakes from his eyelashes.
"We can play as soon as I finish my recycling,
okay?"

In response, the tree's branches
shimmered and sparkled like ice jewels.

Johnny gently lifted the lid of his wooden treasure box, trying hard not to drop his stack of newspapers and crush his new periscope.

"Hey, Tree. Look at this!" Johnny said. "My dad built this new storage box to hold our used newspapers and magazines. After I bring them to the curb, the truck will take all of this paper to the recycling plant."

"There," he said, latching the lid. "Finished. Now we can play!" Johnny hung his periscope on a low branch and stepped back to look at the tree.

"Wow, look at you!" shouted Johnny.
The old oak tree was a majestic king,
dressed in a snow-white robe
and a sparkling, icicle-jeweled crown.
"You even have a castle!"
exclaimed Johnny, pointing
to his tree house.

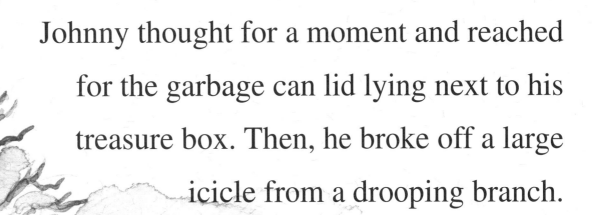

Johnny thought for a moment and reached
for the garbage can lid lying next to his
treasure box. Then, he broke off a large
icicle from a drooping branch.

"I am a brave knight and you are my king," announced Johnny, bowing before the great tree. "Call me Sir Johnny, protector of the land. I have my shield and sword and I am ready to defend our kingdom, Your Majesty."

"Charge!" Johnny shouted as he jumped
onto the back of his loyal horse.

He imagined himself fighting the
trash-breathing dragons at the nearby landfill
where garbage is dumped and buried.
"I am Sir Johnny,
Knight of Recycling!"
he proclaimed.

Suddenly, it stopped snowing
just like that – and all was quiet.

Johnny climbed down from the snowman
and looked around. Had he heard something?
Staying very still, he listened again. Sure enough,
a voice echoed into the frosty air.

Re...cycle...cycle...cycle.

Johnny spun around in surprise. His shield
and frozen sword dropped to the ground.

"Your Majesty ... I mean, Tree ... is that you?"
whispered Johnny.

"Yes, my friend. I am so proud of you for recycling your used paper." Johnny ran to the tree and touched its crisp, ice-covered trunk. On this cold day, Johnny's heart felt warm.

The great oak tree spoke again. "Sir Johnny, recycling happens in a circle of steps and you must complete the circle. You must close the loop." Johnny scratched his head through his snow-crusted hat as snowflakes began falling around him.

"Close the loop?" he asked.
"I thought I knew all the steps of recycling." Using his fingers, hidden within his mittens, Johnny counted the steps as he circled the tree.

I collect the paper, keeping it safe and dry. I bring it to the curb, and then the truck takes it to the recycling plant where it is made into big rolls of new paper. What am I missing?

He plopped down next to the tree and closed his eyes. "When my used paper goes to the recycling plant, new paper is made. I thought that was the last step," he said to himself, putting his mitten to his chin. "The recycling plant..." Johnny repeated. Could the answer be found at the recycling plant?

"What if I were a used newspaper? Then I bet
I could find out about the last step of recycling,"
he thought.

Johnny imagined himself as a newspaper riding
into the recycling plant on top of the recycling truck.

Once inside, he
and the other used
paper from his box
were poured into a
huge blender filled
with water,

where everything
was mashed
into pulp, and
then washed.

Then, Johnny was poured onto a screen and all the water was squeezed out. That tickled and made him giggle!

Next, he was pressed out flat and dried. Johnny was just about to be rolled into new paper when...

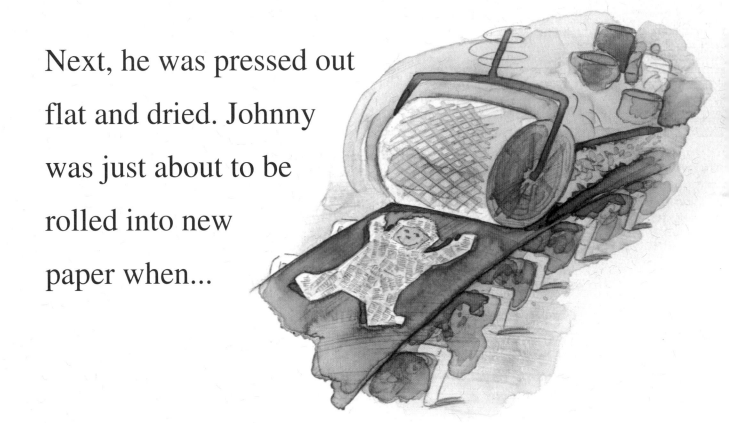

The wind blew hard, and his periscope flew from its branch. Johnny dove into the snow to catch it. As he lay on the fluffy, white ground, Johnny thought and thought about the recycling loop. "A loop is a circle, and the Earth is a circle, too," he said. Then he reached for his periscope and peered up at the clouds.

The blue sky made him think about water.

"The Earth is mostly water," he reminded himself.

"So we must take care of the land we have.

That's why I want to recycle. The Earth doesn't

have room for so many landfills."

He started to make a snow angel as he dreamed on. "I want to learn the last step of recycling so I can keep the trash from going into the land." As he flapped his arms, finishing his snow angel, he noticed something strange in the sky.

Johnny jumped up. "Look at that!" he pointed.

The clouds had taken the shape of arrows.

They were spinning around in circles and

shooting across the sky.

"It looks like fireworks!" he exclaimed.

From high within

the branches of the old oak tree,

the voice came again. "That is the symbol of

the recycling loop, my friend. It tells you the steps

of recycling."

Again there was silence.

Johnny took a good look at the symbol.

"But Tree, I still don't get it. How do I close the loop? How will that symbol up there help me down here?" he asked.

He waited, but there was no answer. Just as quickly and mysteriously as they had appeared, the arrows were gone.

"Was that symbol the last step?" Johnny wondered. He stood there for a moment, poking thoughtfully at the periscope with his ice sword. Suddenly, his eyes grew large as he noticed something familiar on the side of the box. "That's a recycling symbol!" he exclaimed.

Johnny held the
box up to the tree.
"I found it!" he shouted.
"Close the loop – I've got it!
This symbol tells me that
this box is made of
recycled paper. That's
the last step, isn't it?
Using recycled paper."

"First, I save the used paper and put it into my treasure box until it is time to take it to the curb.

"Then, the truck takes it to the recycling plant where it is turned into huge rolls of new paper that are used to form new things like my cereal box.

"And finally, I close the loop by looking for things at the store that have been made from recycled paper. It starts all over again – just like a circle, right?"

The old oak tree swayed proudly and glistened from crown to trunk. "Yes, Johnny, you closed the loop. Choosing to use recycled paper products helps protect the Earth, my friend. It helps fight those trash dragons, too," added the tree happily.

Grasping his sword in one hand and his shield in the other, he proclaimed "I, Sir Johnny, vow to look for the arrows and fight the trash dragons!"

"You, Sir Johnny, are a courageous knight and I am proud to have you protect our kingdom," answered the tree. Johnny smiled as he thought about searching for arrows at the grocery store.

Suddenly, it began to snow heavily and Johnny knew it was time to go inside. "See you tomorrow, Tree," he said, waving goodbye. As he turned to go into the house, he was sure he heard his friend whispering in the wind.

Re ... cycle ... cycle ... cycle

Re ... cycle ... cycle ... cycle ... cycle

With a huge grin, Johnny nodded in agreement and raised his box into the air. "The search for the arrows is on!" he shouted.

Look For These Symbols:

% RECYCLED FIBER

100% RECYCLED FIBER

Get Into The Loop!

Putting your used paper at the curb, or taking it to a drop-off site, is just the beginning of the recycling process. Paper isn't really recycled until companies use it to make new paper products—and people use them. This is called "closing the loop" because it turns recycling into a circle. Paper recycling is easy. Here's how it works:

1. Collecting:

Find out the types of paper your town or school recycles (For example: notebook paper, newspapers, corrugated boxes and paperboard cartons)

▶ Collect and separate paper for recycling

▶ Keep paper clean and free of contaminants such as glass, plastic, food waste and other non-paper items

▶ Separated paper is then picked up by a recycling company

2. Processing:

Collected paper is delivered to a paper mill

▶ At the paper mill, the used paper is mixed with water and made into pulp

▶ The pulp is cleaned, pressed, dried and rolled to make new paper

▶ The new paper is made into new products, such as cereal boxes, notebooks, newspapers, and tissue paper

3. Purchasing:

▶ You can help support paper recycling by buying products made from recycled paper

▶ Read labels for recycled content information and look for these symbols that identify products made from, or packaged in, recycled paper or paperboard

Today, millions of Americans recycle their used home and office papers. In fact, more paper is recycled than all other materials combined. You're probably familiar with the "chasing arrows" symbols, pioneered by the paper industry nearly 30 years ago. These symbols can be found on many different paper products, such as the book you are reading right now.

The recycled paperboard industry turns more than seven million tons of used papers into new 100% recycled paperboard products and packaging every year. More than half the boxed products on store shelves are packaged in 100% recycled paperboard.

% RECYCLED FIBER

This symbol is used when a product or package is made partly of recycled fiber.

100% RECYCLED FIBER

This symbol is used when a product or package is made of 100% recycled fiber.

When you see this symbol you can be sure you're buying a product packaged in 100% recycled paperboard — which is made from the old papers you recycle every day.

Paper Recycling Glossary

Biodegradable
Organic materials such as food scraps, paper and grass clippings that can be broken down by microorganisms into simple compounds (such as carbon dioxide, water or minerals) and become part of the earth again.

Composting
Making rich, new dirt (that will help feed plants) from leaves, grass clippings, soil and water. Paper is compostable. **The paper bag you use to collect leaves is composted with the leaves.**

Contaminant
Any item or material that reduces the quality of paper for recycling. Metal, foil, glass, plastic, and food must be removed from paper before recycling, or they will contaminate the recycling process.

Fiber
Small pieces of thread-like material that are woven together to give structure and strength to paper products. Fiber used in papermaking comes from wood and recovered paper, and sometimes cotton.

Landfill
An enormous pit where trash is buried under shallow layers of dirt. The pit is lined with plastic or clay to prevent the garbage from contaminating groundwater.

Pulp
A watery solution usually made from wood fibers or recovered paper that is used to make new paper.

Recycled Content
The portion of a product or package that contains materials that have been recovered or otherwise diverted from the solid waste stream either during the manufacturing process or after consumer use. Many paper products are made with recycled content.

Paper Recycling
Turning used paper into something new instead of throwing it away. Paper grocery bags, corrugated boxes, newspapers, notebook paper, cereal boxes, envelopes and magazines are just a few of the kinds of paper than can be recycled to make new paper. Most newspapers contain old newspapers that have been recycled and most cereal cartons are made of 100% recycled paperboard.

Renewable Resource
Something that is made by nature and can be used by man and replaced by man, like trees.

Reuse & Recycle

Choose To Reuse.

Think before you throw things away! If an item can be reused for the same purpose, or something else, then reuse it. A paper grocery bag can be reused at least 3 times for groceries, then recycled to make new paper. Paper bags can also be used to make book covers, to wrap presents, to make a hat, or to write on. Can you think of some other uses for paper grocery bags and other items you use everyday?

Something Old... Something New

Paper products can be recycled to make new paper products.

So, recycle your used paper today!

Magazines... newspapers, paper towels, notebook paper, textbook paper

Newspapers... more newspapers, notebook paper, cereal boxes

Paper Grocery Bags... more paper grocery bags, corrugated boxes

Corrugated Boxes... more corrugated boxes, gift boxes

Do Your Bit— Recycle It!

Everyone can make a difference by recycling. Recycling helps conserve natural resources, reduce litter and save landfill space. Fortunately, Americans recycle much more paper than we send to landfills. Kids are doing their part— at home and school—to recycle more used paper. Used paper provides fiber to make new paper, and paper mills are developing new ways to recycle more. Think about the paper products you use everyday. **Which items do you recycle?**

Newspapers: Americans recycle more than 68% of the 62 million newspapers we buy each day. Old newspapers are an important raw material and manufacturers want all they can get to make new newspapers and other paper products.

Paper Grocery Bags: These bags (usually brown) are used to bring home food and other items from the grocery store. They are made of a strong paper, called kraft. They have a flat bottom and straight sides and can be reused at least three times for groceries, then recycled.

Paperboard Cartons: Containers made from layers of paper or paper pulp that have been pressed together to make them strong. Cereal, cookies, cake mixes, laundry soap, video games and pizza all come packaged in paperboard.

Corrugated (cor' ru gāt ed) Boxes: The sturdy brown or white boxes (sometimes called cardboard) used to pack, ship, store and protect items we use every day. Corrugated boxes (the most recycled product in America) are made of several layers of flat paper glued together with a ruffly layer in the middle.

www.earthdaybags.org

Decorate Paper Grocery Bags For Earth Day.

The Earth Day Groceries Project is an easy, fun, and cost-free environmental awareness project that teams up students, teachers and grocers to protect our planet.

The Earth Day Groceries Project helps students develop skills in science, geography, the visual arts, language arts, social studies, and computer science, while empowering them to make a difference in their communities. It generates lively discussions about what items can be recycled and how items we use every day, such as paper grocery bags, can be reused and recycled.

4 Simple Steps

1. Borrow Paper Bags. Teachers borrow a supply of paper grocery bags from a local grocery store.

2. Decorate Paper Grocery Bags. Students decorate the paper bags with colorful environmental messages.

3. Deliver Paper Grocery Bags. Return the decorated bags to the grocery store. On Earth Day (April 22 each year), customers receive their groceries—and the message that kids care about our environment—in the decorated bags.

4. Report Participation on the Web. E-mail a brief report to the project's Web site (www.earthdaybags.org) — detailing how many bags your class or school decorated, along with the name of your participating grocery store. Your bags will be added to the annual tally from around the world.

You've Made a Difference!

In 1999, students at more than 1,000 schools decorated nearly 400,000 paper grocery bags for Earth Day! Each decorated bag is a reminder that kids care about, and are doing their part, to protect our planet. For more details on how your class, school, Scout troop or club can get involved, contact: www.earthdaybags.org. Or, click on the "Kids & Educators" icon on the American Forest & Paper Association Web site at www.afandpa.org.

Kids Take Action!

Hands-On Activities for Teachers and Students

◄ These third grade students from Helen Morgan Elementary in Sparta, NJ helped with the research and development of "Sir Johnny's Recycling Adventures." As part of the research, the class visited a local landfill so students could see what happens to materials that are not recycled. The recycling representative from Sparta visited the school to inform the students about the town's recycling program.

Recycling—See for Yourself.

As part of your educational curriculum on recycling and the environment, consider inviting a representative of your town's recycling center to make a presentation to your students. You might also work with your school's administration to arrange a field trip to a recycling center so students can see how the paper they recycle everyday is turned into new paper, and new products.

For information on recycling facilities and programs in your area, check out the 100% Recycled Paperboard Alliance's Web site at: www.rpa100.com. For information on what items your community recycles, contact the American Forest & Paper Association at: www.afandpa.org.

Does Recycling Really Work?
You bet! Just take a look at this book. It's printed on recycled paper.

When Trash Isn't Trash.

For one day, have students save each of the items they would normally throw away. Have students collect their "trash" in a large plastic bag—and list each of the items they put into the bag on a piece of paper. At the end of the day, have students evaluate which items in their "trash" bag could have been recycled.

Discuss which items are recyclable in your school and community. Could the food items be composted? What about the plastic bag? How can students recycle the paper they used to make their "trash" lists? If a scale is available, have students weigh several of the bags and calculate how many pounds of material the class could save from going to a landfill. By identifying and sorting recyclables, students should see a dramatic difference in how much paper and other materials they actually have to throw away.

. . . Don't Trash Paper Grocery Bags

If you think of a used paper grocery bag as trash, well of course you'll throw it away. A paper grocery bag is a raw material which can be recycled to make new paper.

Recycling Resources

American Forest & Paper Association

www.afandpa.org
America's forest and paper industry is dedicated to Improving Tomorrow's Environment Today. Click on the Kids & Educators icon to access fun facts and activities on paper reuse & recycling and sustainable forestry. For a free Youth Action Kit, contact the Paper Bag Council at (202) 463-2474.

Champion International Corporation

www.championpaper.com
One of the world's largest paper and forest product companies, Champion is committed to sustainable forestry, and to educating the next generation. For information on Champion's efforts to assure long-term productivity and the overall health of the forest ecosystem in its five million acres of forestlands, check out their Web site.

Earth Day Groceries Project®

www.earthdaybags.org
Join thousands of students nationwide in decorating paper grocery bags for Earth Day. Report your participation and view photos and reports from other schools on this interactive Web site. This fun, free environmental education project is effective in enhancing students' skills in computer science, science, geography, language arts, visual arts and environmental stewardship.

Grapevine

grapevine@antiochne.edu
Grapevine, the semi-annual newsletter of the Center for Environmental Education, highlights current and useful environmental curricula, grants and awards, news conferences and other resources. Organizations, publishers and school groups are welcome to submit their stories, events and materials for review and possible inclusion.

Green Brick Road

www.gbr.org
An on-line guide to more than one hundred of the best environmental education resources (including Green Teacher magazine), with detailed descriptions and ordering information.

Hands-On Recycling

mike1rae@aol.com
Invite author Rachael Peterpaul Paulson to your school for an assembly featuring her recycling research. For instructions on how to make recycled paper, see "Johnny and the Old Oak Tree," (Crestmont Publishing, Hands on the World Environmental Series). $10.00, plus shipping. (973) 726-8588.

Kids For A Clean Enviornment (Kids F.A.C.E.®)

www.kidsface.org
Melissa Poe started Kids F.A.C.E. in 1989, when she was nine years old. Now the world's largest youth environmental organization (featuring projects on recycling, tree planting and other environmental issues), Kids F.A.C.E. boasts more than 300,000 members and publishes an online newsletter that reaches millions of young readers.

Project Learning Tree

www.plt.org
This award-winning environmental education program of the American Forest Foundation has served more than 20 million elementary and secondary students worldwide since its inception in 1973. PLT's educational materials encourage youth to explore their environment, to discover original and creative ways to resolve environmental issues, and to get involved in responsible community action projects.

The 100% Recycled Paperboard Alliance

www.rpa100.com
RPA-100% is a group of leading North American recycled paperboard manufacturers representing approximately two-thirds of the industry. For information on recycling facilities and programs in your area, check out their Web site or contact (212) 527-8850.

TREE MUSKETEERS®

800-473-0263
This dynamic "by-kids, for-kids" environmental organization was founded in 1987 by eight-year-old Tara Church and her fellow Girl Scouts. TREE MUSKETEERS empowers and educates kids to make a difference in their communities. The organization has hosted regional and national youth summits, launched a local curbside recycling program and developed a "How To" kit that teaches the basics of tree planting in community settings.

Educational pages designed by Nancy Saiz, Saiz Design

Reprinted with permission of the American Forest & Paper Association (see above).

About the illustrations …

see page 24

see page 11

see page 15

see page 1

see page 35

Some of the illustrations for *Sir Johnny's Recycling Adventure* were inspired by these pictures of Rachael Paulson's children, Danielle and Mikey, playing in the Minnesota snow. The artist read the author's story – then sketched drawings from the above photos to bring the author's words to life. The final illustrations were created using watercolors.

Visit the artist's website at **www.artguys.com**